David Garnett

LADY
INTO
FOX

With Wood Engravings by
R. A. Garnett

Dover Publications, Inc.
Mineola, New York

Bibliographical Note

Lady Into Fox, first published by Dover Publications, Inc., in 2013, is an unabridged republication of the work originally published by Chatto & Windus, London, in 1922. The frontispiece has been moved from its original position to accommodate the pagination for this edition.

Library of Congress Cataloging-in-Publication Data

Garnett, David, 1892–1981.
    Lady into fox / David Garnett ; with wood engravings by R. A. Garnett.
        p. cm.
    ISBN-13: 978-0-486-49319-0
    ISBN-10: 0-486-49319-9
        1. Metamorphosis—Fiction. I. Title.

PR6013.A66L3 2013
823'.912—dc23

2013028949

Manufactured in the United States by RR Donnelley
49319903   2016
www.doverpublications.com

TO
DUNCAN GRANT

MR. AND MRS. TEBRICK AT HOME.

LADY INTO FOX

WONDERFUL or supernatural events are not so uncommon, rather they are irregular in their incidence. Thus there may be not one marvel to speak of in a century, and then often enough comes a plentiful crop of them; monsters of all sorts swarm suddenly upon the earth, comets blaze in the sky, eclipses frighten nature, meteors fall in rain, while mermaids and sirens beguile, and sea-serpents engulf every passing ship, and terrible cataclysms beset humanity.

But the strange event which I shall here relate came alone, unsupported, without companions into a hostile world, and for that very reason claimed little of the general attention of mankind. For the sudden changing of Mrs. Tebrick into a vixen is an established fact which we may attempt to account for as we will. Certainly it is in the explanation of the fact, and the reconciling of it with our general notions that we shall find most difficulty, and not in accepting for true a story which is so fully proved, and that not by one witness but by a dozen, all respectable, and with no possibility of collusion between them.

But here I will confine myself to an exact narrative of the event and all that followed on it. Yet I would not dissuade any of my readers from attempting an explanation of this seeming miracle because up till

now none has been found which is entirely satis-
factory. What adds to the difficulty to my mind is
that the metamorphosis occurred when Mrs. Tebrick
was a full-grown woman, and that it happened suddenly in so short a space of time. The sprouting of
a tail, the gradual extension of hair all over the body,
the slow change of the whole anatomy by a process
of growth, though it would have been monstrous,
would not have been so difficult to reconcile to our
ordinary conceptions, particularly had it happened
in a young child.

But here we have something very different. A
grown lady is changed straightway into a fox. There
is no explaining that away by any natural philosophy.
The materialism of our age will not help us here. It
is indeed *a miracle*; something from outside our
world altogether; an event which we would will-
ingly accept if we were to meet it invested with the
authority of Divine Revelation in the scriptures,
but which we are not prepared to encounter almost
in our time, happening in Oxfordshire amongst our
neighbours.

The only things which go any way towards an
explanation of it are but guesswork, and I give them
more because I would not conceal anything, than
because I think they are of any worth.

Mrs. Tebrick's maiden name was certainly Fox,
and it is possible that such a miracle happening before, the family may have gained their name as a
soubriquet on that account. They were an ancient
family, and have had their seat at Tangley Hall time

out of mind. It is also true that there was a half-tame fox once upon a time chained up at Tangley Hall in the inner yard, and I have heard many speculative wiseacres in the public-houses turn that to great account—though they could not but admit that " there was never one there in Miss Silvia's time." At first I was inclined to think that Silvia Fox, having once hunted when she was a child of ten and having been blooded, might furnish more of an explanation. It seems she took great fright or disgust at it, and vomited after it was done. But now I do not see that it has much bearing on the miracle itself, even though we know that after that she always spoke of the " poor foxes " when a hunt was stirring and never rode to hounds till after her marriage when her husband persuaded her to it.

She was married in the year 1879 to Mr. Richard Tebrick, after a short courtship, and went to live after their honeymoon at Rylands, near Stokoe, Oxon. One point indeed I have not been able to ascertain and that is how they first became acquainted. Tangley Hall is over thirty miles from Stokoe, and is extremely remote. Indeed to this day there is no proper road to it, which is all the more remarkable as it is the principal, and indeed the only, manor house for several miles round.

Whether it was from a chance meeting on the roads, or less romantic but more probable, by Mr. Tebrick becoming acquainted with her uncle, a minor canon at Oxford, and thence being invited by him to visit Tangley Hall, it is impossible to say.

But however they became acquainted the marriage was a very happy one. The bride was in her twenty-third year. She was small, with remarkably small hands and feet. It is perhaps worth noting that there was nothing at all foxy or vixenish in her appearance. On the contrary, she was a more than ordinarily beautiful and agreeable woman. Her eyes were of a clear hazel but exceptionally brilliant, her hair dark, with a shade of red in it, her skin brownish, with a few dark freckles and little moles. In manner she was reserved almost to shyness, but perfectly self-possessed, and perfectly well-bred.

She had been strictly brought up by a woman of excellent principles and considerable attainments, who died a year or so before the marriage. And owing to the circumstance that her mother had been dead many years, and her father bedridden, and not altogether rational for a little while before his death, they had few visitors but her uncle. He often stopped with them a month or two at a stretch, particularly in winter, as he was fond of shooting snipe, which are plentiful in the valley there. That she did not grow up a country hoyden is to be explained by the strictness of her governess and the influence of her uncle. But perhaps living in so wild a place gave her some disposition to wildness, even in spite of her religious upbringing. Her old nurse said : " Miss Silvia was always a little wild at heart," though if this was true it was never seen by anyone else except her husband.

On one of the first days of the year 1880, in the

4

early afternoon, husband and wife went for a walk in the copse on the little hill above Rylands. They were still at this time like lovers in their behaviour and were always together. While they were walking they heard the hounds and later the huntsman's horn in the distance. Mr. Tebrick had persuaded her to hunt on Boxing Day, but with great difficulty, and she had not enjoyed it (though of hacking she was fond enough).

Hearing the hunt, Mr. Tebrick quickened his pace so as to reach the edge of the copse, where they might get a good view of the hounds if they came that way. His wife hung back, and he, holding her hand, began almost to drag her. Before they gained the edge of the copse she suddenly snatched her hand away from his very violently and cried out, so that he instantly turned his head.

Where his wife had been the moment before was a small fox, of a very bright red. It looked at him very beseechingly, advanced towards him a pace or two, and he saw at once that his wife was looking at him from the animal's eyes. You may well think if he were aghast : and so maybe was his lady at finding herself in that shape, so they did nothing for nearly half-an-hour but stare at each other, he bewildered, she asking him with her eyes as if indeed she spoke to him : " What am I now become ? Have pity on me, husband, have pity on me for I am your wife."

So that with his gazing on her and knowing her well, even in such a shape, yet asking himself at

5

every moment : " Can it be she ? Am I not dreaming ? " and her beseeching and lastly fawning on him and seeming to tell him that it was she indeed, they came at last together and he took her in his arms. She lay very close to him, nestling under his coat and fell to licking his face, but never taking her eyes from his.

The husband all this while kept turning the thing in his head and gazing on her, but he could make no sense of what had happened, but only comforted himself with the hope that this was but a momentary change, and that presently she would turn back again into the wife that was one flesh with him.

One fancy that came to him, because he was so much more like a lover than a husband, was that it was his fault, and this because if anything dreadful happened he could never blame her but himself for it.

So they passed a good while, till at last the tears welled up in the poor fox's eyes and she began weeping (but quite in silence), and she trembled too as if she were in a fever. At this he could not contain his own tears, but sat down on the ground and sobbed for a great while, but between his sobs kissing her quite as if she had been a woman, and not caring in his grief that he was kissing a fox on the muzzle.

They sat thus till it was getting near dusk, when he recollected himself, and the next thing was that he must somehow hide her, and then bring her home.

He waited till it was quite dark that he might the better bring her into her own house without being seen, and buttoned her inside his topcoat, nay, even in his passion tearing open his waistcoat and his shirt that she might lie the closer to his heart. For when we are overcome with the greatest sorrow we act not like men or women but like children whose comfort in all their troubles is to press themselves against their mother's breast, or if she be not there to hold each other tight in one another's arms.

When it was dark he brought her in with infinite precautions, yet not without the dogs scenting her, after which nothing could moderate their clamour.

Having got her into the house, the next thing he thought of was to hide her from the servants. He carried her to the bedroom in his arms and then went downstairs again.

Mr. Tebrick had three servants living in the house, the cook, the parlourmaid, and an old woman who had been his wife's nurse. Besides these women there was a groom or a gardener (whichever you choose to call him), who was a single man and so lived out, lodging with a labouring family about half a mile away.

Mr. Tebrick going downstairs pitched upon the parlourmaid.

" Janet," says he, " Mrs. Tebrick and I have had some bad news, and Mrs. Tebrick was called away instantly to London and left this afternoon, and I am staying to-night to put our affairs in order. We are shutting up the house, and I must give you and

Mrs. Brant a month's wages and ask you to leave to-morrow morning at seven o'clock. We shall probably go away to the Continent, and I do not know when we shall come back. Please tell the others, and now get me my tea and bring it into my study on a tray."

Janet said nothing for she was a shy girl, particularly before gentlemen, but when she entered the kitchen Mr. Tebrick heard a sudden burst of conversation with many exclamations from the cook.

When she came back with his tea, Mr. Tebrick said : " I shall not require you upstairs. Pack your own things and tell James to have the waggonette ready for you by seven o'clock to-morrow morning to take you to the station. I am busy now, but I will see you again before you go."

When she had gone Mr. Tebrick took the tray upstairs. For the first moment he thought the room was empty, and his vixen got away, for he could see no sign of her anywhere. But after a moment he saw something stirring in a corner of the room, and then behold ! she came forth dragging her dressing-gown, into which she had somehow struggled.

This must surely have been a comical sight, but poor Mr. Tebrick was altogether too distressed then or at any time afterwards to divert himself at such ludicrous scenes. He only called to her softly :

" Silvia—Silvia. What do you do there ? " And then in a moment saw for himself what she would be at, and began once more to blame himself heartily —because he had not guessed that his wife would

8

not like to go naked, no notwithstanding the shape she was in. Nothing would satisfy him then till he had clothed her suitably, bringing her dresses from the wardrobe for her to choose. But as might have been expected, they were too big for her now, but at last he picked out a little dressing-jacket that she was fond of wearing sometimes in the mornings. It was made of a flowered silk, trimmed with lace, and the sleeves short enough to sit very well on her now. While he tied the ribands his poor lady thanked him with gentle looks and not without some modesty and confusion. He propped her up in an armchair with some cushions, and they took tea together, she very delicately drinking from a saucer and taking bread and butter from his hands. All this showed him, or so he thought, that his wife was still herself ; there was so little wildness in her demeanour and so much delicacy and decency, especially in her not wishing to run naked, that he was very much comforted, and began to fancy they could be happy enough if they could escape the world and live always alone.

From this too sanguine dream he was aroused by hearing the gardener speaking to the dogs, trying to quiet them, for ever since he had come in with his vixen they had been whining, barking and growling, and all as he knew because there was a fox within doors and they would kill it.

He started up now, calling to the gardener that he would come down to the dogs himself to quiet them, and bade the man go indoors again and leave it to him. All this he said in a dry, compelling kind of voice which made the fellow do as he was bid, though it was against his will, for he was curious. Mr. Tebrick went downstairs, and taking his gun from the rack loaded it and went out into the yard. Now there were two dogs, one a handsome Irish setter that was his wife's dog (she had brought it with her from Tangley Hall on her marriage) ; the other was an old fox terrier called Nelly that he had had ten years or more.

When he came out into the yard both dogs saluted him by barking and whining twice as much as they did before, the setter jumping up and down at the end of his chain in a frenzy, and Nelly shivering, wagging her tail, and looking first at her master and then at the house door, where she could smell the fox right enough.

There was a bright moon, so that Mr. Tebrick could see the dogs as clearly as could be. First he shot his wife's setter dead, and then looked about him for Nelly to give her the other barrel, but he could see her nowhere. The bitch was clean gone, till, looking to see how she had broken her chain, he found her lying hid in the back of her kennel. But that trick did not save her, for Mr. Tebrick, after trying to pull her out by her chain and finding it useless—she would not come,—thrust the muzzle of his gun into the kennel, pressed it into her body and so shot her. Afterwards, striking a match, he looked in at her to make certain she was dead. Then, leaving the dogs as they were, chained up, Mr.

Tebrick went indoors again and found the gardener, who had not yet gone home, gave him a month's wages in lieu of notice and told him he had a job for him yet—to bury the two dogs and that he should do it that same night.

But by all this going on with so much strangeness and authority on his part, as it seemed to them, the servants were much troubled. Hearing the shots while he was out in the yard his wife's old nurse, or Nanny, ran up to the bedroom though she had no business there, and so opening the door saw the poor fox dressed in my lady's little jacket lying back in the cushions, and in such a reverie of woe that she heard nothing.

Old Nanny, though she was not expecting to find her mistress there, having been told that she was

11

gone that afternoon to London, knew her instantly, and cried out :

" Oh, my poor precious ! Oh, poor Miss Silvia ! What dreadful change is this ? " Then, seeing her mistress start and look at her, she cried out :

" But never fear, my darling, it will all come right, your old Nanny knows you, it will all come right in the end."

But though she said this she did not care to look again, and kept her eyes turned away so as not to meet the foxy slit ones of her mistress, for that was too much for her. So she hurried out soon, fearing to be found there by Mr. Tebrick, and who knows, perhaps shot, like the dogs, for knowing the secret.

Mr. Tebrick had all this time gone about paying off his servants and shooting his dogs as if he were in a dream. Now he fortified himself with two or three glasses of strong whisky and went to bed, taking his vixen into his arms, where he slept soundly. Whether she did or not is more than I or anybody else can say.

In the morning when he woke up they had the place to themselves, for on his instructions the servants had all left first thing : Janet and the cook to Oxford, where they would try and find new places, and Nanny going back to the cottage near Tangley, where her son lived, who was the pigman there.

So with that morning there began what was now to be their ordinary life together. He would get up when it was broad day, and first thing light the fire downstairs and cook the breakfast, then brush his wife, sponge her with a damp sponge, then brush her again, in all this using scent very freely to hide somewhat her rank odour. When she was dressed he carried her downstairs and they had their breakfast together, she sitting up to table with him, drinking her saucer of tea, and taking her food from his fingers, or at any rate being fed by him. She was still fond of the same food that she had been used to before her transformation, a lightly boiled egg or slice of ham, a piece of buttered toast or two, with a little quince and apple jam. While I am on the subject of her food, I should say that reading in the encyclopedia he found that foxes on the Continent are inordinately fond of grapes, and that during the autumn season they abandon their ordinary diet for them, and then grow exceedingly fat and lose their offensive odour.

This appetite for grapes is so well confirmed by Æsop, and by passages in the Scriptures, that it is strange Mr. Tebrick should not have known it. After reading this account he wrote to London for a basket of grapes to be posted to him twice a week and was rejoiced to find that the account in the encyclopedia was true in the most important of these particulars. His vixen relished them exceedingly and seemed never to tire of them, so that he increased his order first from one pound to three pounds and afterwards to five. Her odour abated so much by this means that he came not to notice it at all except sometimes in the mornings before her toilet.

What helped most to make living with her bearable for him was that she understood him perfectly —yes, every word he said, and though she was dumb she expressed herself very fluently by looks and signs though never by the voice.

Thus he frequently conversed with her, telling her all his thoughts and hiding nothing from her, and this the more readily because he was very quick to catch her meaning and her answers.

" Puss, Puss," he would say to her, for calling her that had been a habit with him always. " Sweet Puss, some men would pity me living alone here with you after what has happened, but I would not change places while you were living with any man for the whole world. Though you are a fox I would rather live with you than any woman. I swear I would, and that too if you were changed to anything." But then, catching her grave look, he would say : " Do you think I jest on these things, my dear ? I do not. I swear to you, my darling, that all my life I will be true to you, will be faithful, will respect and reverence you who are my wife. And I will do that not because of any hope that God in His mercy will see fit to restore your shape, but solely because I love you. However you may be changed, my love is not."

Then anyone seeing them would have sworn that they were lovers, so passionately did each look on the other.

Often he would swear to her that the devil might have power to work some miracles, but that he would find it beyond him to change his love for her.

These passionate speeches, however they might have struck his wife in an ordinary way, now seemed to be her chief comfort. She would come to him, put her paw in his hand and look at him with sparkling eyes shining with joy and gratitude, would pant with eagerness, jump at him and lick his face.

Now he had many little things which busied him in the house—getting his meals, setting the room straight, making the bed and so forth. When he was doing this housework it was comical to watch his vixen. Often she was as it were beside herself with vexation and distress to see him in his clumsy way doing what she could have done so much better had she been able. Then, forgetful of the decency and the decorum which she had at first imposed upon herself never to run upon all fours, she followed him everywhere, and if he did one thing wrong she stopped him and showed him the way of it. When he had forgot the hour for his meal she would come and tug his sleeve and tell him as if she spoke : " Husband, are we to have no luncheon to-day ? "

This womanliness in her never failed to delight him, for it showed she was still his wife, buried as it were in the carcase of a beast but with a woman's soul. This encouraged him so much that he debated with himself whether he should not read aloud to her, as he often had done formerly. At last, since he could find no reason against it, he went to the shelf and fetched down a volume of the " History of

Clarissa Harlowe," which he had begun to read aloud to her a few weeks before. He opened the volume where he had left off, with Lovelace's letter after he had spent the night waiting fruitlessly in the copse.

" *Good God !*

What is now to become of me ?

My feet benumbed by midnight wanderings through the heaviest dews that ever fell ; my wig and my linen dripping with the hoarfrost dissolving on them !

Day but just breaking . . . " etc.

While he read he was conscious of holding her attention, then after a few pages the story claimed all his, so that he read on for about half-an-hour without looking at her. When he did so he saw that she was not listening to him, but was watching something with strange eagerness. Such a fixed intent look was on her face that he was alarmed and sought the cause of it. Presently he found that her gaze was fixed on the movements of her pet dove which was in its cage hanging in the window. He spoke to her, but she seemed displeased, so he laid " Clarissa Harlowe " aside. Nor did he ever repeat the experiment of reading to her.

Yet that same evening, as he happened to be looking through his writing table drawer with Puss beside him looking over his elbow, she spied a pack of cards, and then he was forced to pick them out to please her, then draw them from their case. At last, trying first one thing, then another, he found that what she was after was to play piquet with him. They

16

had some difficulty at first in contriving for her to hold her cards and then to play them, but this was at last overcome by his stacking them for her on a sloping board, after which she could flip them out very neatly with her claws as she wanted to play them. When they had overcome this trouble they played three games, and most heartily she seemed to enjoy them. Moreover she won all three of them. After this they often played a quiet game of piquet together, and cribbage too. I should say that in marking the points at cribbage on the board he always moved her pegs for her as well as his own, for she could not handle them or set them in the holes.

The weather, which had been damp and misty, with frequent downpours of rain, improved very much in the following week, and, as often happens in January, there were several days with the sun shining, no wind and light frosts at night, these frosts becoming more intense as the days went on till bye and bye they began to think of snow.

With this spell of fine weather it was but natural that Mr. Tebrick should think of taking his vixen out of doors. This was something he had not yet done, both because of the damp rainy weather up till then and because the mere notion of taking her out filled him with alarm. Indeed he had so many apprehensions beforehand that at one time he resolved totally against it. For his mind was filled not only with the fear that she might escape from him and run away, which he knew was groundless, but with more rational visions, such as wandering curs, traps, gins, spring guns, besides a dread of being seen with her by the neighbourhood. At last however he resolved on it, and all the more as his vixen kept asking him in the gentlest way : " Might she not go out into the garden ? " Yet she always listened very submissively when he told her that he was afraid if they were seen together it would excite the curiosity of their neighbours ; besides this, he often told her of his fears for her on account of dogs. But one day she answered this by leading him into the hall and pointing boldly to his gun. After this he resolved to take her, though with full precautions. That is he left the house door open so that in case of need she could beat a swift retreat, then he took his gun under his arm, and lastly he had her well wrapped up in a little fur jacket lest she should take cold.

He would have carried her too, but that she delicately disengaged herself from his arms and looked at him very expressively to say that she would go by herself. For already her first horror of being seen to go upon all fours was worn off ; reasoning no doubt upon it, that either she must resign herself to go that way or else stay bed-ridden all the rest of her life.

Her joy at going into the garden was inexpressible. First she ran this way, then that, though keeping always close to him, looking very sharply with ears cocked forward first at one thing, then another and then up to catch his eye.

For some time indeed she was almost dancing

with delight, running round him, then forward a yard or two, then back to him and gambolling beside him as they went round the garden. But in spite of her joy she was full of fear. At every noise, a cow lowing, a cock crowing, or a ploughman in the distance hulloaing to scare the rooks, she started, her ears pricked to catch the sound, her muzzle wrinkled up and her nose twitched, and she would then press herself against his legs. They walked round the garden and down to the pond where there were ornamental waterfowl, teal, widgeon and mandarin ducks, and seeing these again gave her great pleasure. They had always been her favourites, and now she was so overjoyed to see them that she behaved with very little of her usual self-restraint. First she stared at them, then bouncing up to her husband's knee sought to kindle an equal excitement in his mind. Whilst she rested her paws on his knee she turned her head again and again towards the ducks as though she could not take her eyes off them, and then ran down before him to the water's edge.

19

But her appearance threw the ducks into the utmost degree of consternation. Those on shore or near the bank swam or flew to the centre of the pond, and there huddled in a bunch; and then, swimming round and round, they began such a quacking that Mr. Tebrick was nearly deafened. As I have before said, nothing in the ludicrous way that arose out of the metamorphosis of his wife (and such incidents were plentiful) ever stood a chance of being smiled at by him. So in this case, too, for realising that the silly ducks thought his wife a fox indeed and were alarmed on that account he found painful that spectacle which to others might have been amusing.

Not so his vixen, who appeared if anything more pleased than ever when she saw in what a commotion she had set them, and began cutting a thousand pretty capers. Though at first he called to her to come back and walk another way, Mr. Tebrick was overborne by her pleasure and sat down, while she frisked around him happier far than he had seen her ever since the change. First she ran up to him in a laughing way, all smiles, and then ran down again to the water's edge and began frisking and frolicking, chasing her own brush, dancing on her hind legs even, and rolling on the ground, then fell to running in circles, but all this without paying any heed to the ducks.

But they, with their necks craned out all pointing one way, swam to and fro in the middle of the pond, never stopping their quack, quack quack, and keeping time too, for they all quacked in chorus. Presently she came further away from the pond, and he, thinking they had had enough of this sort of entertainment, laid hold of her and said to her :

" Come, Silvia, my dear, it is growing cold, and it is time we went indoors. I am sure taking the air has done you a world of good, but we must not linger any more."

She appeared then to agree with him, though she threw half a glance over her shoulder at the ducks, and they both walked soberly enough towards the house.

When they had gone about halfway she suddenly slipped round and was off. He turned quickly and saw the ducks had been following them.

So she drove them before her back into the pond, the ducks running in terror from her with their wings spread, and she not pressing them, for he saw that had she been so minded she could have caught two or three of the nearest. Then, with her brush waving above her, she came gambolling back to him so playfully that he stroked her indulgently, though he was first vexed, and then rather puzzled that his wife should amuse herself with such pranks.

But when they got within doors he picked her up in his arms, kissed her and spoke to her.

" Silvia, what a light-hearted childish creature you are. Your courage under misfortune shall be a lesson to me, but I cannot, I cannot bear to see it."

Here the tears stood suddenly in his eyes, and he lay down upon the ottoman and wept, paying no heed to her until presently he was aroused by her licking his cheek and his ear.

After tea she led him to the drawing room and scratched at the door till he opened it, for this was part of the house which he had shut up, thinking three or four rooms enough for them now, and to save the dusting of it. Then it seemed she would have him play to her on the pianoforte : she led him to it, nay, what is more, she would herself pick out the music he was to play. First it was a fugue of Handel's, then one of Mendelssohn's Songs Without Words, and then " The Diver," and then music from Gilbert and Sullivan ; but each piece of music she picked out was gayer than the last one. Thus they sat happily engrossed for perhaps an hour in the candle light until the extreme cold in that unwarmed room stopped his playing and drove them downstairs to the fire. Thus did she admirably comfort her husband when he was dispirited.

Yet next morning when he woke he was distressed when he found that she was not in the bed with him but was lying curled up at the foot of it. During breakfast she hardly listened when he spoke, and then impatiently, but sat staring at the dove.

Mr. Tebrick sat silently looking out of window for some time, then he took out his pocket book ; in it there was a photograph of his wife taken soon after their wedding. Now he gazed and gazed upon those familiar features, and now he lifted his head and looked at the animal before him. He laughed

then bitterly, the first and last time for that matter
that Mr. Tebrick ever laughed at his wife's transformation, for he was not very humorous. But this
laugh was sour and painful to him. Then he tore up
the photograph into little pieces, and scattered them
out of the window, saying to himself : " Memories
will not help me here," and turning to the vixen he
saw that she was still staring at the caged bird, and
as he looked he saw her lick her chops.

He took the bird into the next room, then acting
suddenly upon the impulse, he opened the cage door
and set it free, saying as he did so :

" Go, poor bird ! Fly from this wretched house
while you still remember your mistress who fed you
from her coral lips. You are not a fit plaything for
her now. Farewell, poor bird ! Farewell ! Unless,"
he added with a melancholy smile, " you return
with good tidings like Noah's dove."

But, poor gentleman, his troubles were not over
yet, and indeed one may say that he ran to meet
them by his constant supposing that his lady should
still be the same to a tittle in her behaviour now that
she was changed into a fox.

Without making any unwarrantable suppositions
as to her soul or what had now become of it (though
we could find a good deal to the purpose on that
point in the system of Paracelsus), let us consider
only how much the change in her body must needs
affect her ordinary conduct. So that before we judge
too harshly of this unfortunate lady, we must reflect
upon the physical necessities and infirmities and

appetites of her new condition, and we must magnify the fortitude of her mind which enabled her to behave with decorum, cleanliness and decency in spite of her new situation.

Thus she might have been expected to befoul her room, yet never could anyone, whether man or beast, have shown more nicety in such matters. But at luncheon Mr. Tebrick helped her to a wing of chicken, and leaving the room for a minute to fetch some water which he had forgot, found her at his return on the table crunching the very bones. He stood silent, dismayed and wounded to the heart at this sight. For we must observe that this unfortunate husband thought always of his vixen as that gentle and delicate woman whom she had lately been. So that whenever his vixen's conduct went beyond that which he expected in his wife he was, as it were, cut to the quick, and no kind of agony could be greater to him than to see her thus forget herself. On this account it may indeed be regretted that Mrs. Tebrick had been so exactly well-bred, and in particular that her table manners had always been scrupulous. Had she been in the habit, like a continental princess I have dined with, of taking her leg of chicken by the drumstick and gnawing the flesh, it had been far better for him now. But as her manners had been perfect, so the lapse of them was proportionately painful to him. Thus in this instance he stood as it were in silent agony till she had finished her hideous crunching of the chicken bones and had devoured every scrap. Then he spoke to her gently, taking her on to his knee, stroking her fur and fed her with a few grapes, saying to her :

" Silvia, Silvia, is it so hard for you ? Try and remember the past, my darling, and by living with me we will quite forget that you are no longer a woman. Surely this affliction will pass soon, as suddenly as it came, and it will all seem to us like an evil dream."

Yet though she appeared perfectly sensible of his words and gave him sorrowful and penitent looks like her old self, that same afternoon, on taking her out, he had all the difficulty in the world to keep her from going near the ducks.

There came to him then a thought that was very disagreeable to him, namely, that he dare not trust his wife alone with any bird or she would kill it. And this was the more shocking to him to think of since it meant that he durst not trust her as much as a dog even. For we may trust dogs who are familiars, with all the household pets ; nay more, we can put them upon trust with anything and know they will not touch it, not even if they be starving. But things were come to such a pass with his vixen that he dared not in his heart trust her at all. Yet she was still in many ways so much more woman than fox that he could talk to her on any subject and she would understand him, better far than the oriental women who are kept in subjection can ever understand their masters unless they converse on the most trifling household topics.

Thus she understood excellently well the importance and duties of religion. She would listen

with approval in the evening when he said the Lord's
Prayer, and was rigid in her observance of the
Sabbath. Indeed, the next day being Sunday he,
thinking no harm, proposed their usual game of
piquet, but no, she would not play. Mr. Tebrick,
not understanding at first what she meant, though
he was usually very quick with her, he proposed it
to her again, which she again refused, and this time,
to show her meaning, made the sign of the cross
with her paw. This exceedingly rejoiced and comforted him in his distress. He begged her pardon,
and fervently thanked God for having so good a
wife, who, in spite of all, knew more of her
duty to God than he did. But here I must warn the
reader from inferring that she was a papist because
she then made the sign of the cross. She made that
sign to my thinking only on compulsion because
she could not express herself except in that way.
For she had been brought up as a true Protestant,
and that she still was one is confirmed by her ob-
jection to cards, which would have been less than
nothing to her had she been a papist. Yet that evening, taking her into the drawing room so that he
might play her some sacred music, he found her after
some time cowering away from him in the farthest
corner of the room, her ears flattened back and an
expression of the greatest anguish in her eyes. When
he spoke to her she licked his hand, but remained
shivering for a long time at his feet and showed the
clearest symptoms of terror if he so much as moved
towards the piano.

On seeing this and recollecting how ill the ears of a dog can bear with our music, and how this dislike might be expected to be even greater in a fox, all of whose senses are more acute from being a wild creature, recollecting this he closed the piano and taking her in his arms, locked up the room and never went into it again. He could not help marvelling though, since it was but two days after she had herself led him there, and even picked out for him to play and sing those pieces which were her favourites.

That night she would not sleep with him, neither in the bed nor on it, so that he was forced to let her curl herself up on the floor. But neither would she sleep there, for several times she woke him by trotting around the room, and once when he had got sound asleep by springing on the bed and then off it, so that he woke with a violent start and cried out, but got no answer either, except hearing her trotting round and round the room. Presently he imagines to himself that she must want something, and so fetches her food and water, but she never so much as looks at it, but still goes on her rounds, every now and then scratching at the door.

Though he spoke to her, calling her by her name, she would pay no heed to him, or else only for the moment. At last he gave her up and said to her plainly : " The fit is on you now Silvia to be a fox, but I shall keep you close and in the morning you will recollect yourself and thank me for having kept you now."

So he lay down again, but not to sleep, only to

listen to his wife running about the room and trying to get out of it. Thus he spent what was perhaps the most miserable night of his existence. In the morning she was still restless, and was reluctant to let him wash and brush her, and appeared to dislike being scented but as it were to bear with it for his sake. Ordinarily she had taken the greatest pleasure imaginable in her toilet, so that on this account, added to his sleepless night, Mr. Tebrick was utterly dejected, and it was then that he resolved to put a project into execution that would show him, so he thought, whether he had a wife or only a wild vixen in his house. But yet he was comforted that she bore at all with him, though so restlessly that he did not spare her, calling her a " bad wild fox." And then speaking to her in this manner : " Are you not ashamed, Silvia, to be such a madcap, such a wicked hoyden ? You who were particular in dress. I see it was all vanity—now you have not your former advantages you think nothing of decency."

His words had some effect with her too, and with himself, so that by the time he had finished dressing her they were both in the lowest state of spirits imaginable and neither of them far from tears.

Breakfast she took soberly enough, and after that he went about getting his experiment ready, which was this. In the garden he gathered together a nosegay of snowdrops, those being all the flowers he could find, and then going into the village of Stokoe bought a Dutch rabbit (that is a black and white one) from a man there who kept them.

When he got back he took her flowers and at the same time set down the basket with the rabbit in it, with the lid open. Then he called to her : " Silvia, I have brought some flowers for you. Look, the first snowdrops."

At this she ran up very prettily, and never giving as much as one glance at the rabbit which had hopped out of its basket, she began to thank him for the flowers. Indeed she seemed indefatigable in shewing her gratitude, smelt them, stood a little way off looking at them, then thanked him again. Mr. Tebrick (and this was all part of his plan) then took a vase and went to find some water for them, but left the flowers beside her. He stopped away five minutes, timing it by his watch and listening very intently, but never heard the rabbit squeak. Yet when he went in what a horrid shambles was spread before his eyes. Blood on the carpet, blood on the armchairs and antimacassars, even a little blood spurtled on to the wall, and what was worse, Mrs. Tebrick tearing and growling over a piece of the skin and the legs, for she had eaten up all the rest of it. The poor

gentleman was so heartbroken over this that he was
like to have done himself an injury, and at one
moment thought of getting his gun, to have shot
himself and his vixen too. Indeed the extremity of
his grief was such that it served him a very good
turn, for he was so entirely unmanned by it that for
some time he could do nothing but weep, and fell
into a chair with his head in his hands, and so kept
weeping and groaning.

After he had been some little while employed in
this dismal way, his vixen, who had by this time
bolted down the rabbit skin, head, ears and all, came
to him and putting her paws on his knees, thrust
her long muzzle into his face and began licking him.
But he, looking at her now with different eyes, and
seeing her jaws still sprinkled with fresh blood and
her claws full of the rabbit's fleck, would have none
of it.

But though he beat her off four or five times even
to giving her blows and kicks, she still came back to
him, crawling on her belly and imploring his for-
giveness with wide-open sorrowful eyes. Before he
had made this rash experiment of the rabbit and the
flowers, he had promised himself that if she failed
in it he would have no more feeling or compassion
for her than if she were in truth a wild vixen out of
the woods. This resolution, though the reasons for
it had seemed to him so very plain before, he now
found more difficult to carry out than to decide on.
At length after cursing her and beating her off for
upwards of half-an-hour, he admitted to himself

that he still did care for her, and even loved her dearly in spite of all, whatever pretence he affected towards her. When he had acknowledged this he looked up at her and met her eyes fixed upon him, and held out his arms to her and said :

" Oh Silvia, Silvia, would you had never done this ! Would I had never tempted you in a fatal hour ! Does not this butchery and eating of raw meat and rabbit's fur disgust you ? Are you a monster in your soul as well as in your body ? Have you forgotten what it is to be a woman ? "

Meanwhile, with every word of his, she crawled a step nearer on her belly and at last climbed sorrowfully into his arms. His words then seemed to take effect on her and her eyes filled with tears and she wept most penitently in his arms, and her body shook with her sobs as if her heart were breaking. This sorrow of hers gave him the strangest mixture of pain and joy that he had ever known, for his love for her returning with a rush, he could not bear to witness her pain and yet must take pleasure in it as it fed his hopes of her one day returning to be a woman. So the more anguish of shame his vixen underwent, the greater his hopes rose, till his love and pity for her increasing equally, he was almost wishing her to be nothing more than a mere fox than to suffer so much by being half-human.

At last he looked about him somewhat dazed with so much weeping, then set his vixen down on the ottoman, and began to clean up the room with a heavy heart. He fetched a pail of water and washed

out all the stains of blood, gathered up the two antimacassars and fetched clean ones from the other
rooms. While he went about this work his vixen sat
and watched him very contritely with her nose
between her two front paws, and when he had done
he brought in some luncheon for himself, though it
was already late, but none for her, she having lately
so infamously feasted. But water he gave her and a
bunch of grapes. Afterwards she led him to the small
tortoiseshell cabinet and would have him open it.
When he had done so she motioned to the portable

stereoscope which lay inside. Mr. Tebrick instantly
fell in with her wish and after a few trials adjusted
it to her vision. Thus they spent the rest of the afternoon together very happily looking through the

collection of views which he had purchased, of Italy, Spain and Scotland. This diversion gave her great apparent pleasure and afforded him considerable comfort. But that night he could not prevail upon her to sleep in bed with him, and finally allowed her to sleep on a mat beside the bed where he could stretch down and touch her. So they passed the night, with his hand upon her head.

The next morning he had more of a struggle than ever to wash and dress her. Indeed at one time nothing but holding her by the scruff prevented her from getting away from him, but at last he achieved his object and she was washed, brushed, scented and dressed, although to be sure this left him better pleased than her, for she regarded her silk jacket with disfavour.

Still at breakfast she was well mannered though a trifle hasty with her food. Then his difficulties with her began for she would go out, but as he had his housework to do, he could not allow it. He brought her picture books to divert her, but she would have none of them but stayed at the door scratching it with her claws industriously till she had worn away the paint.

At first he tried coaxing her and wheedling, gave her cards to play patience and so on, but finding nothing would distract her from going out, his temper began to rise, and he told her plainly that she must wait his pleasure and that he had as much natural obstinacy as she had. But to all that he said she paid no heed whatever but only scratched the harder.

Thus he let her continue until luncheon, when she would not sit up, or eat off a plate, but first was for getting on to the table, and when that was prevented, snatched her meat and ate it under the table. To all his rebukes she turned a deaf or sullen ear, and so they each finished their meal eating little, either of them, for till she would sit at table he would give her no more, and his vexation had taken away his own appetite. In the afternoon he took her out for her airing in the garden.

She made no pretence now of enjoying the first snowdrops or the view from the terrace. No—there was only one thing for her now—the ducks, and she was off to them before he could stop her. Luckily they were all swimming when she got there (for a stream running into the pond on the far side it was not frozen there).

When he had got down to the pond, she ran out on to the ice, which would not bear his weight, and though he called her and begged her to come back she would not heed him but stayed frisking about, getting as near the ducks as she dared, but being circumspect in venturing on to the thin ice.

Presently she turned on herself and began tearing off her clothes, and at last by biting got off her little jacket and taking it in her mouth stuffed it into a hole in the ice where he could not get it. Then she ran hither and thither a stark naked vixen, and without giving a glance to her poor husband who stood silently now upon the bank, with despair and terror settled in his mind. She let him stay there most

of the afternoon till he was chilled through and
through and worn out with watching her. At last he
reflected how she had just stripped herself and how
in the morning she struggled against being dressed,
and he thought perhaps he was too strict with her
and if he let her have her own way they could manage
to be happy somehow together even if she did eat
off the floor. So he called out to her then :

" Silvia, come now, be good, you shan't wear any
more clothes if you don't want to, and you needn't
sit at table neither, I promise. You shall do as you
like in that, but you must give up one thing, and
that is you must stay with me and not go out alone,
for that is dangerous. If any dog came on you he
would kill you."

Directly he had finished speaking she came to him
joyously, began fawning on him and prancing round
him so that in spite of his vexation with her, and
being cold, he could not help stroking her.

" Oh, Silvia, are you not wilful and cunning ? I
see you glory in being so, but I shall not reproach
you but shall stick to my side of the bargain, and
you must stick to yours."

He built a big fire when he came back to the house
and took a glass or two of spirits also, to warm himself up, for he was chilled to the very bone. Then,
after they had dined, to cheer himself he took another
glass, and then another, and so on till he was very
merry, he thought. Then he would play with his
vixen, she encouraging him with her pretty sportive-
ness. He got up to catch her then and finding

35

himself unsteady on his legs, he went down on to all fours. The long and the short of it is that by drinking he drowned all his sorrow ; and then would be a beast too like his wife, though she was one through no fault of her own, and could not help it. To what lengths he went then in that drunken humour I shall not offend my readers by relating, but shall only say that he was so drunk and sottish that he had a very imperfect recollection of what had passed when he woke the next morning. There is no exception to the rule that if a man drink heavily at night the next morning will show the other side to his nature. Thus with Mr. Tebrick, for as he had been beastly, merry and a very dare-devil the night before, so on his awakening was he ashamed, melancholic and a true penitent before his Creator. The first thing he did when he came to himself was to call out to God to forgive him for his sin, then he fell into earnest prayer and continued so for half-an-hour upon his knees. Then he got up and dressed but continued very melancholy for the whole of the morning. Being in this mood you may imagine it hurt him to see his wife running about naked, but he reflected it would be a bad reformation that began with breaking faith. He had made a bargain and he would stick to it, and so he let her be, though sorely against his will.

For the same reason, that is because he would stick to his side of the bargain, he did not require her to sit up at table, but gave her her breakfast on a dish in the corner, where to tell the truth she on her side ate it all up with great daintiness and propriety. Nor she did make any attempt to go out of doors that morning, but lay curled up in an armchair before the fire dozing. After lunch he took her out, and she never so much as offered to go near the ducks, but running before him led him on to take her a longer walk. This he consented to do very much to her joy and delight. He took her through the fields by the most unfrequented ways, being much alarmed lest they should be seen by anyone. But by good luck they walked above four miles across country and saw nobody. All the way his wife kept running on ahead of him, and then back to him to lick his hand and so on, and appeared delighted at taking exercise. And though they started two or three rabbits and a hare in the course of their walk she never attempted to go after them, only giving them a look and then looking back to him, laughing at him as it were for his warning cry of " Puss ! come in, no nonsense now ! "

Just when they got home and were going into the porch they came face to face with an old woman. Mr. Tebrick stopped short in consternation and looked about for his vixen, but she had run forward without any shyness to greet her. Then he recognised the intruder, it was his wife's old nurse.

" What are you doing here, Mrs. Cork ? " he asked her.

Mrs. Cork answered him in these words :

" Poor thing. Poor Miss Silvia ! It is a shame to let her run about like a dog. It is a shame, and your own wife too. But whatever she looks like, you should trust her the same as ever. If you do she'll do her best to be a good wife to you, if you don't I shouldn't wonder if she did turn into a proper fox. I saw her, sir, before I left, and I've had no peace of mind. I couldn't sleep thinking of her. So I've come back to look after her, as I have done all her life, sir," and she stooped down and took Mrs. Tebrick by the paw.

Mr. Tebrick unlocked the door and they went in. When Mrs. Cork saw the house she exclaimed again and again : " The place was a pigstye. They couldn't live like that, a gentleman must have somebody to look after him. She would do it. He could trust her with the secret."

Had the old woman come the day before it is likely enough that Mr. Tebrick would have sent her packing. But the voice of conscience being woken in him by his drunkenness of the night before he was heartily ashamed of his own management of the business, moreover the old woman's words that " it was a shame to let her run about like a dog," moved him exceedingly. Being in this mood the truth is he welcomed her.

But we may conclude that Mrs. Tebrick was as sorry to see her old Nanny as her husband was glad. If we consider that she had been brought up strictly by her when she was a child, and was now again in her power, and that her old nurse could never be satisfied with her now whatever she did, but would always think her wicked to be a fox at all, there seems good reason for her dislike. And it is possible, too, that there may have been another cause as well, and that is jealousy. We know her husband was always trying to bring her back to be a woman, or at any rate to get her to act like one, may she not have been hoping to get him to be like a beast himself or to act like one ? May she not have thought it easier to change him thus than ever to change herself back into being a woman ? If we think that she had had a success of this kind only the night before, when he got drunk, can we not conclude that this was indeed the case, and then we have another good reason why the poor lady should hate to see her old nurse ?

It is certain that whatever hopes Mr. Tebrick had of Mrs. Cork affecting his wife for the better were disappointed. She grew steadily wilder and after a few days so intractable with her that Mr. Tebrick again took her under his complete control.

The first morning Mrs. Cork made her a new jacket, cutting down the sleeves of a blue silk one of Mrs. Tebrick's and trimming it with swan's down, and directly she had altered it, put it on her mistress, and fetching a mirror would have her admire the fit of it. All the time she waited on Mrs. Tebrick the old woman talked to her as though she were a baby, and treated her as such, never thinking perhaps that she was either the one thing or the other, that is either a lady to whom she owed respect and who had rational powers exceeding her own, or else a wild creature on whom words were wasted. But though at first she submitted passively, Mrs. Tebrick only waited for her Nanny's back to be turned to tear up her pretty piece of handiwork into shreds, and then ran gaily about waving her brush with only a few ribands still hanging from her neck.

So it was time after time (for the old woman was used to having her own way) until Mrs. Cork would, I think, have tried punishing her if she had not been afraid of Mrs. Tebrick's rows of white teeth, which she often showed her, then laughing afterwards, as if to say it was only play.

Not content with tearing off the dresses that were fitted on her, one day Silvia slipped upstairs to her wardrobe and tore down all her old dresses and made havoc with them, not sparing her wedding dress either, but tearing and ripping them all up so that there was hardly a shred or rag left big enough to dress a doll in. On this, Mr. Tebrick, who had let the old woman have most of her management to see what she could make of her, took her back under his own control.

He was sorry enough now that Mrs. Cork had disappointed him in the hopes he had had of her, to have the old woman, as it were, on his hands. True she could be useful enough in many ways to him, by doing the housework, the cooking and mending, but still he was anxious since his secret was in her keeping, and the more now that she had tried her hand with his wife and failed. For he saw that vanity had kept her mouth shut if she had won over her mistress to better ways, and her love for her would have grown by getting her own way with her. But now that she had failed she bore her mistress a grudge for not being won over, or at the best was become indifferent to the business, so that she might very readily blab.

For the moment all Mr. Tebrick could do was to keep her from going into Stokoe to the village, where she would meet all her old cronies and where there were certain to be any number of inquiries about what was going on at Rylands and so on. But as he saw that it was clearly beyond his power, however vigilant he might be, to watch over the old woman and his wife, and to prevent anyone from meeting with either of them, he began to consider what he could best do.

Since he had sent away his servants and the gardener, giving out a story of having received bad news and his wife going away to London where he would join her, their probably going out of England and so on, he knew well enough that there would be a great deal of talk in the neighbourhood.

And as he had now stayed on, contrary to what he had said, there would be further rumour. Indeed, had he known it, there was a story already going round the country that his wife had run away with Major Solmes, and that he was gone mad with grief, that he had shot his dogs and his horses and shut himself up alone in the house and would speak with no one. This story was made up by his neighbours not because they were fanciful or wanted to deceive, but like most tittle-tattle to fill a gap, as few like to confess ignorance, and if people are asked about such or such a man they must have something to say, or they suffer in everybody's opinion, are set down as dull or "out of the swim." In this way I met not long ago with someone who, after talking some little while and not knowing me or who I was, told me that David Garnett was dead, and died of being bitten by a cat after he had tormented it. He had long grown a nuisance to his friends as an exorbitant sponge upon them, and the world was well rid of him.

Hearing this story of myself diverted me at the time, but I fully believe it has served me in good stead since. For it set me on my guard as perhaps nothing else would have done, against accepting for true all floating rumour and village gossip, so that now I am by second nature a true sceptic and scarcely believe anything unless the evidence for it is conclusive. Indeed I could never have got to the bottom of this history if I had believed one tenth part of what I was told, there was so much of it that was either manifestly false and absurd, or else contradictory to the ascertained facts. It is therefore only the bare bones of the story which you will find written here, for I have rejected all the flowery embroideries which would be entertaining reading enough, I daresay, for some, but if there be any doubt of the truth of a thing it is poor sort of entertainment to read about in my opinion.

To get back to our story : Mr. Tebrick having considered how much the appetite of his neighbours would be whetted to find out the mystery by his remaining in that part of the country, determined that the best thing he could do was to remove.

After some time turning the thing over in his mind, he decided that no place would be so good for his purpose as old Nanny's cottage. It was thirty miles away from Stokoe, which in the country means as far as Timbuctoo does to us in London. Then it was near Tangley, and his lady having known it from her childhood would feel at home there, and also it was utterly remote, there being no village near it or manor house other than Tangley Hall, which was now untenanted for the greater part of the year. Nor did it mean imparting his secret to others, for there was only Mrs. Cork's son, a widower, who being out at work all day would be easily outwitted, the more so as he was stone deaf and of a slow and saturnine disposition. To be sure there was little Polly, Mrs. Cork's granddaughter, but either Mr. Tebrick forgot her altogether, or else reckoned her as a mere baby and not to be thought of as a danger.

He talked the thing over with Mrs. Cork, and they decided upon it out of hand. The truth is the old woman was beginning to regret that her love and her curiosity had ever brought her back to Rylands, since so far she had got much work and little credit by it.

When it was settled, Mr. Tebrick disposed of the remaining business he had at Rylands in the afternoon, and that was chiefly putting out his wife's riding horse into the keeping of a farmer near by, for he thought he would drive over with his own

43

horse, and the other spare horse tandem in the dog-cart.

The next morning they locked up the house and they departed, having first secured Mrs. Tebrick in a large wicker hamper where she would be tolerably comfortable. This was for safety, for in the agitation of driving she might jump out, and on the other hand, if a dog scented her and she were loose, she might be in danger of her life. Mr. Tebrick drove with the hamper beside him on the front seat, and spoke to her gently very often.

She was overcome by the excitement of the journey and kept poking her nose first through one crevice, then through another, turning and twisting the whole time and peeping out to see what they were passing. It was a bitterly cold day, and when they had gone about fifteen miles they drew up by the roadside to rest the horses and have their own luncheon, for he dared not stop at an inn. He knew that any living creature in a hamper, even if it be only an old fowl, always draws attention; there would be several loafers most likely who would notice that he had a fox with him, and even if he left the hamper in the cart the dogs at the inn would be sure to sniff out her scent. So not to take any chances he drew up at the side of the road and rested there, though it was freezing hard and a north-east wind howling.

He took down his precious hamper, unharnessed his two horses, covered them with rugs and gave them their corn. Then he opened the basket and let his wife out. She was quite beside herself with joy,

44

running hither and thither, bouncing up on him, looking about her and even rolling over on the ground. Mr. Tebrick took this to mean that she was glad at making this journey and rejoiced equally with her. As for Mrs. Cork, she sat motionless on the back seat of the dogcart well wrapped up, eating her sandwiches, but would not speak a word. When they had stayed there half-an-hour Mr. Tebrick harnessed the horses again, though he was so cold he could scarcely buckle the straps, and put his vixen in her basket, but seeing that she wanted to look about her, he let her tear away the osiers with her teeth till she had made a hole big enough for her to put her head out of.

They drove on again and then the snow began to come down and that in earnest, so that he began to be afraid they would never cover the ground. But just after nightfall they got in, and he was content to leave unharnessing the horses and baiting them to Simon, Mrs. Cork's son. His vixen was tired by then, as well as he, and they slept together, he in the bed and she under it, very contentedly.

The next morning he looked about him at the place and found the thing there that he most wanted, and that was a little walled-in garden where his wife could run in freedom and yet be in safety.

After they had had breakfast she was wild to go out into the snow. So they went out together, and he had never seen such a mad creature in all his life as his wife was then. For she ran to and fro as if she were crazy, biting at the snow and rolling in it, and round and round in circles and rushed back at him fiercely as if she meant to bite him. He joined her in the frolic, and began snowballing her till she was so wild that it was all he could do to quiet her again and bring her indoors for luncheon. Indeed with her gambollings she tracked the whole garden over with her feet; he could see where she had rolled in the snow and where she had danced in it, and looking at those prints of her feet as they went in, made his heart ache, he knew not why.

They passed the first day at old Nanny's cottage happily enough, without their usual bickerings, and this because of the novelty of the snow which had diverted them. In the afternoon he first showed his wife to little Polly, who eyed her very curiously but hung back shyly and seemed a good deal afraid of the fox. But Mr. Tebrick took up a book and let them get acquainted by themselves, and presently looking up saw that they had come together and Polly was stroking his wife, patting her and running her fingers through her fur. Presently she began talking to the fox, and then brought her doll in to show her so that very soon they were very good playmates together. Watching the two gave Mr. Tebrick great delight, and in particular when he noticed that there was something very motherly in his vixen. She was indeed far above the child in intelligence and restrained herself too from any hasty action. But while she seemed to wait on Polly's pleasure yet she managed to give a twist to the game, whatever it was, that never failed to delight the

46

little girl. In short, in a very little while, Polly was so taken with her new playmate that she cried when she was parted from her and wanted her always with her. This disposition of Mrs. Tebrick's made Mrs. Cork more agreeable than she had been lately either to the husband or the wife.

Three days after they had come to the cottage the weather changed, and they woke up one morning to find the snow gone, and the wind in the south, and the sun shining, so that it was like the first beginning of spring.

Mr. Tebrick let his vixen out into the garden after

breakfast, stayed with her awhile, and then went indoors to write some letters.

When he got out again he could see no sign of her anywhere, so that he ran about bewildered, calling to her. At last he spied a mound of fresh earth by the wall in one corner of the garden, and running thither found that there was a hole freshly dug seeming to go under the wall. On this he ran out of the garden quickly till he came to the other side of the wall, but there was no hole there, so he concluded that she was not yet got through. So it proved to be, for reaching down into the hole he felt her brush with his hand, and could hear her distinctly working away with her claws. He called to her then, saying : " Silvia, Silvia, why do you do this ? Are you trying to escape from me ? I am your husband, and if I keep you confined it is to protect you, not to let you run into danger. Show me how I can make you happy and I will do it, but do not try to escape from me. I love you, Silvia ; is it because of that that you want to fly from me to go into the world where you will be in danger of your life always ? There are dogs everywhere and they all would kill you if it were not for me. Come out, Silvia, come out."

But Silvia would not listen to him, so he waited there silent. Then he spoke to her in a different way, asking her had she forgot the bargain she made with him that she would not go out alone, but now when she had all the liberty of a garden to herself would she wantonly break her word ? And he asked her, were they not married ? And had she not always

48

LADY INTO FOX

found him a good husband to her ? But she heeded this neither until presently his temper getting somewhat out of hand he cursed her obstinacy and told her if she would be a damned fox she was welcome to it, for his part he could get his own way. She had not escaped yet. He would dig her out for he still had time, and if she struggled put her in a bag.

These words brought her forth instantly and she looked at him with as much astonishment as if she knew not what could have made him angry. Yes, she even fawned on him, but in a good-natured kind of way, as if she were a very good wife putting up wonderfully with her husband's temper.

These airs of hers made the poor gentleman (so simple was he) repent his outburst and feel most ashamed.

But for all that when she was out of the hole he filled it up with great stones and beat them in with a crowbar so she should find her work at that point harder than before if she was tempted to begin it again.

In the afternoon he let her go again into the garden but sent little Polly with her to keep her company. But presently on looking out he saw his vixen had climbed up into the limbs of an old pear tree and was looking over the wall, and was not so far from it but she might jump over it if she could get a little further.

Mr. Tebrick ran out into the garden as quick as he could, and when his wife saw him it seemed she was startled and made a false spring at the wall, so

49

that she missed reaching it and fell back heavily to the ground and lay there insensible. When Mr. Tebrick got up to her he found her head was twisted under her by her fall and the neck seemed to be broken. The shock was so great to him that for some time he could not do anything, but knelt beside her turning her limp body stupidly in his hands. At length he recognised that she was indeed dead, and beginning to consider what dreadful afflictions God had visited him with, he blasphemed horribly and called on God to strike him dead, or give his wife back to him.

" Is it not enough," he cried, adding a foul blasphemous oath, " that you should rob me of my dear wife, making her a fox, but now you must rob me of that fox too, that has been my only solace and comfort in this affliction ? "

Then he burst into tears and began wringing his hands and continued there in such an extremity of grief for half-an-hour that he cared nothing, neither what he was doing, nor what would become of him in the future, but only knew that his life was ended now and he would not live any longer than he could help.

All this while the little girl Polly stood by, first staring, then asking him what had happened, and lastly crying with fear, but he never heeded her nor looked at her but only tore his hair, sometimes shouted at God, or shook his fist at Heaven. So in a fright Polly opened the door and ran out of the garden.

At length worn out, and as it were all numb with

his loss, Mr. Tebrick got up and went within doors, leaving his dear fox lying near where she had fallen.

He stayed indoors only two minutes and then came out again with a razor in his hand intending to cut his own throat, for he was out of his senses in this first paroxysm of grief.

But his vixen was gone, at which he looked about for a moment bewildered, and then enraged, thinking that somebody must have taken the body.

The door of the garden being open he ran straight through it. Now this door, which had been left ajar by Polly when she ran off, opened into a little court-yard where the fowls were shut in at night; the woodhouse and the privy also stood there. On the far side of it from the garden gate were two large wooden doors big enough when open to let a cart enter, and high enough to keep a man from looking over into the yard.

When Mr. Tebrick got into the yard he found his vixen leaping up at these doors, and wild with terror, but as lively as ever he saw her in his life. He ran up to her but she shrank away from him, and would then have dodged him too, but he caught hold of her. She bared her teeth at him but he paid no heed to that, only picked her straight up into his arms and took her so indoors. Yet all the while he could scarce believe his eyes to see her living, and felt her all over very carefully to find if she had not some bones broken. But no, he could find none. Indeed it was some hours before this poor silly gentleman began to suspect the truth, which was that his vixen had practised a deception upon him, and all the time he was bemoaning his loss in such heartrending terms, she was only shamming death to run away directly she was able. If it had not been that the yard gates were shut, which was a mere chance, she had got her liberty by that trick. And that this was only a trick of hers to sham dead was plain when he had thought it over. Indeed it is an old and time-honoured trick of the fox. It is in Æsop and a hundred other writers have confirmed it since. But so thoroughly had he been deceived by her, that at first he was as much overcome with joy at his wife still being alive, as he had been with grief a little while before, thinking her dead.

He took her in his arms, hugging her to him and thanking God a dozen times for her preservation. But his kissing and fondling her had very little effect now, for she did not answer him by licking or soft looks, but stayed huddled up and sullen, with her hair bristling on her neck and her ears laid back every time he touched her. At first he thought this might be because he had touched some broken bone or tender place where she had been hurt, but at last the truth came to him.

Thus he was again to suffer, and though the pain of knowing her treachery to him was nothing to the grief of losing her, yet it was more insidious and lasting. At first, from a mere nothing, this pain grew gradually until it was a torture to him. If he had been one of your stock ordinary husbands, such a one who by experience has learnt never to enquire too closely into his wife's doings, her comings or goings, and never to ask her, " How she has spent the day ? " for fear he should be made the more of a fool, had Mr. Tebrick been such a one he had been luckier, and his pain would have been almost nothing. But you must consider that he had never been deceived once by his wife in the course of their married life. No, she had never told him as much as one white lie, but had always been frank, open and ingenuous as if she and her husband were not husband and wife, or indeed of opposite sexes. Yet we must rate him as very foolish, that living thus with a fox, which beast has the same reputation for deceitfulness, craft and cunning, in all countries, all ages, and amongst all races of mankind, he should expect this fox to be as candid and honest with him in all things as the country girl he had married.

His wife's sullenness and bad temper continued that day, for she cowered away from him and hid under the sofa, nor could he persuade her to come out from there. Even when it was her dinner time she stayed, refusing resolutely to be tempted out with food, and lying so quiet that he heard nothing from her for hours. At night he carried her up to the bedroom, but she was still sullen and refused to eat a morsel, though she drank a little water during the night, when she fancied he was asleep.

The next morning was the same, and by now Mr. Tebrick had been through all the agonies of wounded self-esteem, disillusionment and despair that a man can suffer. But though his emotions rose up in his heart and nearly stifled him he showed no sign of them to her, neither did he abate one jot his tenderness and consideration for his vixen. At breakfast he tempted her with a freshly killed young pullet. It hurt him to make this advance to her, for hitherto he had kept her strictly on cooked meats, but the pain of seeing her refuse it was harder still for him to bear. Added to this was now an anxiety lest she should starve herself to death rather than stay with him any longer.

All that morning he kept her close, but in the afternoon let her loose again in the garden after he had lopped the pear tree so that she could not repeat her performance of climbing.

But seeing how disgustedly she looked while he was by, never offering to run or to play as she was used, but only standing stock still with her tail between her legs, her ears flattened, and the hair bristling on her shoulders, seeing this he left her to herself out of mere humanity.

When he came out after half-an-hour he found that she was gone, but there was a fair sized hole by the wall, and she just buried all but her brush, digging desperately to get under the wall and make her escape.

He ran up to the hole, and put his arm in after her and called to her to come out, but she would not. So at first he began pulling her out by the shoulder, then his hold slipping, by the hind legs. As soon as he had drawn her forth she whipped round and snapped at his hand and bit it through near the joint of the thumb, but let it go instantly.

They stayed there for a minute facing each other, he on his knees and she facing him the picture of unrepentant wickedness and fury. Being thus on his knees, Mr. Tebrick was down on her level very nearly, and her muzzle was thrust almost into his face. Her ears lay flat on her head, her gums were bared in a silent snarl, and all her beautiful teeth threatening him that she would bite him again. Her back too was half-arched, all her hair bristling and her brush held drooping. But it was her eyes that held his, with their slit pupils looking at him with savage desperation and rage.

The blood ran very freely from his hand but he never noticed that or the pain of it either, for all his thoughts were for his wife.

" What is this, Silvia ? " he said very quietly, " what is this ? Why are you so savage now ? If I stand between you and your freedom it is because I love you. Is it such torment to be with me ? " But Silvia never stirred a muscle.

" You would not do this if you were not in anguish, poor beast, you want your freedom. I cannot keep you, I cannot hold you to vows made when you were a woman. Why, you have forgotten who I am."

The tears then began running down his cheeks, he sobbed, and said to her :

" Go—I shall not keep you. Poor beast, poor beast, I love you, I love you. Go if you want to. But if you remember me come back. I shall never keep you against your will. Go—go. But kiss me now."

He leant forward then and put his lips to her

snarling fangs, but though she kept snarling she did not bite him. Then he got up quickly and went to the door of the garden that opened into a little paddock against a wood.

When he opened it she went through it like an arrow, crossed the paddock like a puff of smoke and in a moment was gone from his sight. Then, suddenly finding himself alone, Mr. Tebrick came as it were to himself and ran after her, calling her by name and shouting to her, and so went plunging into the wood, and through it for about a mile, running almost blindly.

At last when he was worn out he sat down, seeing that she had gone beyond recovery and it was already night. Then, rising, he walked slowly homewards, wearied and spent in spirit. As he went he bound up his hand that was still running with blood. His coat was torn, his hat lost, and his face scratched right across with briars. Now in cold blood he began to reflect on what he had done and to repent bitterly having set his wife free. He had betrayed her so that now, from his act, she must lead the life of a wild fox for ever, and must undergo all the rigours and hardships of the climate, and all the hazards of a hunted creature. When Mr. Tebrick got back to the cottage he found Mrs. Cork was sitting up for him. It was already late.

" What have you done with Mrs. Tebrick, sir ? I missed her, and I missed you, and I have not known what to do, expecting something dreadful had happened. I have been sitting up for you half the night. And where is she now, sir ? "

She accosted him so vigorously that Mr. Tebrick stood silent. At length he said : " I have let her go. She has run away."

" Poor Miss Silvia ! " cried the old woman. " Poor creature ! You ought to be ashamed, sir ! Let her go indeed ! Poor lady, is that the way for her husband to talk ! It is a disgrace. But I saw it coming from the first."

The old woman was white with fury, she did not mind what she said, but Mr. Tebrick was not listening to her. At last he looked at her and saw that she had just begun to cry, so he went out of the room and up to bed, and lay down as he was, in his clothes, utterly exhausted, and fell into a dog's sleep, starting up every now and then with horror, and then falling back with fatigue. It was late when he woke up, but cold and raw, and he felt cramped in all his limbs. As he lay he heard again the noise which had woken him—the trotting of several horses, and the voices of men riding by the house. Mr. Tebrick jumped up and ran to the window and then looked out, and the first thing that he saw was a gentleman in a pink coat riding at a walk down the lane. At this sight Mr. Tebrick waited no longer, but pulling on his boots in mad haste, ran out instantly, meaning to say that they must not hunt, and how his wife was escaped and they might kill her.

But when he found himself outside the cottage words failed him and fury took possession of him, so that he could only cry out :

" How dare you, you damned blackguard ? "

And so, with a stick in his hand, he threw himself on the gentleman in the pink coat and seized his horse's rein, and catching the gentleman by the leg was trying to throw him. But really it is impossible to say what Mr. Tebrick intended by his behaviour or what he would have done, for the gentleman finding himself suddenly assaulted in so unexpected a fashion by so strange a touzled and dishevelled figure, clubbed his hunting crop and dealt him a blow on the temple so that he fell insensible.

Another gentleman rode up at this moment and they were civil enough to dismount and carry Mr. Tebrick into the cottage, where they were met by old Nanny who kept wringing her hands and told them Mr. Tebrick's wife had run away and she was a vixen, and that was the cause that Mr. Tebrick had run out and assaulted them.

The two gentlemen could not help laughing at this, and mounting their horses rode on without delay, after telling each other that Mr. Tebrick, whoever he was, was certainly a madman, and the old woman seemed as mad as her master.

This story, however, went the rounds of the gentry in those parts and perfectly confirmed everyone in their previous opinion, namely that Mr. Tebrick was mad and his wife had run away from him. The part about her being a vixen was laughed at by the few that heard it, but was soon left out as immaterial to the story, and incredible in itself, though afterwards it came to be remembered and its significance to be understood.

When Mr. Tebrick came to himself it was past noon, and his head was aching so painfully that he could only call to mind in a confused way what had happened.

However, he sent off Mrs. Cork's son directly on one of his horses to enquire about the hunt.

At the same time he gave orders to old Nanny that she was to put out food and water for her mistress, on the chance that she might yet be in the neighbourhood.

By nightfall Simon was back with the news that the hunt had had a very long run but had lost one fox, then, drawing a covert, had chopped an old dog fox, and so ended the day's sport.

This put poor Mr. Tebrick in some hopes again, and he rose at once from his bed, and went out to the wood and began calling his wife, but was overcome with faintness, and lay down and so passed the night in the open, from mere weakness.

In the morning he got back again to the cottage but he had taken a chill, and so had to keep his bed for three or four days after.

All this time he had food put out for her every night, but though rats came to it and ate of it, there were never any prints of a fox.

At last his anxiety began working another way, that is he came to think it possible that his vixen would have gone back to Stokoe, so he had his horses harnessed in the dogcart and brought to the door and then drove over to Rylands, though he was still in a fever, and with a heavy cold upon him.

LADY INTO FOX

After that he lived always solitary, keeping away from his fellows and only seeing one man, called Askew, who had been brought up a jockey at Wantage, but was grown too big for his profession. He mounted this loafing fellow on one of his horses three days a week and had him follow the hunt and report to him whenever they killed, and if he could view the fox so much the better, and then he made him describe it minutely, so he should know if it were his Silvia. But he dared not trust himself to go himself, lest his passion should master him and he might commit a murder.

Every time there was a hunt in the neighbourhood he set the gates wide open at Rylands and the house doors also, and taking his gun stood sentinel in the hope that his wife would run in if she were pressed by the hounds, and so he could save her. But only once a hunt came near, when two foxhounds that had lost the main pack strayed on to his land and he shot them instantly and buried them afterwards himself.

It was not long now to the end of the season, as it was the middle of March.

But living as he did at this time, Mr. Tebrick grew more and more to be a true misanthrope. He denied admittance to any that came to visit him, and rarely showed himself to his fellows, but went out chiefly in the early mornings before people were about, in the hope of seeing his beloved fox. Indeed it was only this hope that he would see her again that kept him alive, for he had become so careless of

his own comfort in every way that he very seldom
ate a proper meal, taking no more than a crust of
bread with a morsel of cheese in the whole day,
though sometimes he would drink half a bottle of
whiskey to drown his sorrow and to get off to sleep,
for sleep fled from him, and no sooner did he begin
dozing but he awoke with a start thinking he had
heard something. He let his beard grow too, and
though he had always been very particular in his
person before, he now was utterly careless of it,
gave up washing himself for a week or two at a
stretch, and if there was dirt under his finger nails
let it stop there.

All this disorder fed a malignant pleasure in him.
For by now he had come to hate his fellow men and
was embittered against all human decencies and
decorum. For strange to tell he never once in these
months regretted his dear wife whom he had so much
loved. No, all that he grieved for now was his departed vixen. He was haunted all this time not by
the memory of a sweet and gentle woman, but by
the recollection of an animal ; a beast it is true that
could sit at table and play piquet when it would,
but for all that nothing really but a wild beast. His
one hope now was the recovery of this beast, and of
this he dreamed continually. Likewise both waking
and sleeping he was visited by visions of her ; her
mask, her full white-tagged brush, white throat, and
the thick fur in her ears all haunted him.

Every one of her foxey ways was now so abso-
lutely precious to him that I believe that if he had

known for certain she was dead, and had thoughts of marrying a second time, he would never have been happy with a woman. No, indeed, he would have been more tempted to get himself a tame fox, and would have counted that as good a marriage as he could make.

Yet this all proceeded one may say from a passion, and a true conjugal fidelity, that it would be hard to find matched in this world. And though we may think him a fool, almost a madman, we must, when we look closer, find much to respect in his extraordinary devotion. How different indeed was he from those who, if their wives go mad, shut them in madhouses and give themselves up to concubinage, and nay, what is more, there are many who extenuate such conduct too. But Mr. Tebrick was of a very different temper, and though his wife was now nothing but a hunted beast, cared for no one in the world but her.

But this devouring love ate into him like a consumption, so that by sleepless nights, and not caring for his person, in a few months he was worn to the shadow of himself. His cheeks were sunk in, his eyes hollow but excessively brilliant, and his whole body had lost flesh, so that looking at him the wonder was that he was still alive.

Now that the hunting season was over he had less anxiety for her, yet even so he was not positive that the hounds had not got her. For between the time of his setting her free, and the end of the hunting season (just after Easter), there were but three vixens killed near. Of those three one was a half-blind or wall-eyed, and one was a very grey dull-coloured beast. The third answered more to the description of his wife, but that it had not much black on the legs, whereas in her the blackness of the legs was very plain to be noticed. But yet his fear made him think that perhaps she had got mired in running and the legs being muddy were not remarked on as black.

One morning the first week in May, about four o'clock, when he was out waiting in the little copse, he sat down for a while on a tree stump, and when he looked up saw a fox coming towards him over the ploughed field. It was carrying a hare over its shoulder so that it was nearly all hidden from him. At last, when it was not twenty yards from him, it crossed over, going into the copse, when Mr. Tebrick stood up and cried out, " Silvia, Silvia, is it you ? "

The fox dropped the hare out of his mouth and stood looking at him, and then our gentleman saw at the first glance that this was not his wife. For whereas Mrs. Tebrick had been of a very bright red, this was a swarthier duller beast altogether, more-over it was a good deal larger and higher at the shoulder and had a great white tag to his brush. But the fox after the first instant did not stand for his portrait you may be sure, but picked up his hare and made off like an arrow.

Then Mr. Tebrick cried out to himself : " Indeed I am crazy now ! My affliction has made me lose what little reason I ever had. Here am I taking every fox I see to be my wife ! My neighbours call me a madman and now I see that they are right. Look at me now, oh God ! How foul a creature I am. I hate my fellows. I am thin and wasted by this consuming passion, my reason is gone and I feed myself on dreams. Recall me to my duty, bring me back to decency, let me not become a beast likewise, but restore me and forgive me, Oh my Lord."

With that he burst into scalding tears and knelt down and prayed, a thing he had not done for many weeks.

When he rose up he walked back feeling giddy and exceedingly weak, but with a contrite heart, and then washed himself thoroughly and changed his clothes, but his weakness increasing he lay down for the rest of the day, but read in the Book of Job and was much comforted.

For several days after this he lived very soberly, for his weakness continued, but every day he read in the bible, and prayed earnestly, so that his resolution was so much strengthened that he determined to overcome his folly, or his passion, if he could, and at any rate to live the rest of his life very religiously. So strong was this desire in him to amend his ways that he considered if he should not go to spread the Gospel abroad, for the Bible Society, and so spend the rest of his days.

Indeed he began a letter to his wife's uncle, the canon, and he was writing this when he was startled by hearing a fox bark.

Yet so great was this new turn he had taken that

he did not rush out at once, as he would have done before, but stayed where he was and finished his letter.

Afterwards he said to himself that it was only a wild fox and sent by the devil to mock him, and that madness lay that way if he should listen. But on the other hand he could not deny to himself that it might have been his wife, and that he ought to welcome the prodigal. Thus he was torn between these two thoughts, neither of which did he completely believe. He stayed thus tormented with doubts and fears all night.

The next morning he woke suddenly with a start and on the instant heard a fox bark once more. At that he pulled on his clothes and ran out as fast as he could to the garden gate. The sun was not yet high, the dew thick everywhere, and for a minute or two everything was very silent. He looked about him eagerly but could see no fox, yet there was already joy in his heart.

Then while he looked up and down the road, he saw his vixen step out of the copse about thirty yards away. He called to her at once.

" My dearest wife ! Oh, Silvia ! You are come back ! " and at the sound of his voice he saw her wag her tail, which set his last doubts at rest.

But then though he called her again, she stepped into the copse once more though she looked back at him over her shoulder as she went. At this he ran after her, but softly and not too fast lest he should frighten her away, and then looked about for her

66

again and called to her when he saw her among the
trees still keeping her distance from him. He followed
her then, and as he approached so she retreated from
him, yet always looking back at him several times.

He followed after her through the underwood up
the side of the hill, when suddenly she disappeared
from his sight, behind some bracken.

When he got there he could see her nowhere, but
looking about him found a fox's earth, but so well
hidden that he might have passed it by a thousand
times and would never have found it unless he had
made particular search at that spot.

But now, though he went on his hands and knees,
he could see nothing of his vixen, so that he waited
a little while wondering.

Presently he heard a noise of something moving
in the earth, and so waited silently, then saw something which pushed itself into sight. It was a small
sooty black beast, like a puppy. There came another
behind it, then another and so on till there were five
of them. Lastly there came his vixen pushing her
litter before her, and while he looked at her silently,
a prey to his confused and unhappy emotions, he saw
that her eyes were shining with pride and happiness.

She picked up one of her youngsters then, in her
mouth, and brought it to him and laid it in front of
him, and then looked up at him very excited, or so
it seemed.

Mr. Tebrick took the cub in his hands, stroked it
and put it against his cheek. It was a little fellow with
a smutty face and paws, with staring vacant eyes of

a brilliant electric blue and a little tail like a carrot. When he was put down he took a step towards his mother and then sat down very comically.

Mr. Tebrick looked at his wife again and spoke to her, calling her a good creature. Already he was resigned and now, indeed, for the first time he thoroughly understood what had happened to her, and how far apart they were now. But looking first at one cub, then at another, and having them sprawling over his lap, he forgot himself, only watching the pretty scene, and taking pleasure in it. Now and then he would stroke his vixen and kiss her, liberties which she freely allowed him. He marvelled more than ever now at her beauty ; for her gentleness with the cubs and the extreme delight she took in them seemed to him then to make her more lovely than before. Thus lying amongst them at the mouth of the earth he idled away the whole of the morning.

First he would play with one, then with another, rolling them over and tickling them, but they were too young yet to lend themselves to any other more active sport than this. Every now and then he would

stroke his vixen, or look at her, and thus the time slipped away quite fast and he was surprised when she gathered her cubs together and pushed them before her into the earth, then coming back to him once or twice very humanly bid him " Good-bye and that she hoped she would see him soon again, now he had found out the way."

So admirably did she express her meaning that it would have been superfluous for her to have spoken had she been able, and Mr. Tebrick, who was used to her, got up at once and went home.

But now that he was alone, all the feelings which he had not troubled himself with when he was with her, but had, as it were, put aside till after his innocent pleasures were over, all these came swarming back to assail him in a hundred tormenting ways.

Firstly he asked himself : Was not his wife unfaithful to him, had she not prostituted herself to a beast ? Could he still love her after that ? But this did not trouble him so much as it might have done. For now he was convinced inwardly that she could no longer in fairness be judged as a woman, but as a fox only. And as a fox she had done no more than other foxes, indeed in having cubs and tending them with love, she had done well.

Whether in this conclusion Mr. Tebrick was in the right or not, is not for us here to consider. But I would only say to those who would censure him for a too lenient view of the religious side of the matter, that we have not seen the thing as he did, and perhaps if it were displayed before our eyes we might be led to the same conclusions.

This was, however, not a tenth part of the trouble in which Mr. Tebrick found himself. For he asked himself also : " Was he not jealous ? " And looking into his heart he found that he was indeed jealous, yes, and angry too, that now he must share his vixen with wild foxes. Then he questioned himself if it were not dishonourable to do so, and whether he should not utterly forget her and follow his original intention of retiring from the world, and see her no more.

Thus he tormented himself for the rest of that day, and by evening he had resolved never to see her again.

But in the middle of the night he woke up with his head very clear, and said to himself in wonder, " Am I not a madman ? I torment myself foolishly with fantastic notions. Can a man have his honour sullied by a beast ? I am a man, I am immeasurably superior to the animals. Can my dignity allow of my being jealous of a beast ? A thousand times no. Were I to lust after a vixen, I were a criminal indeed. I can be happy in seeing my vixen, for I love her, but she does right to be happy according to the laws of her being."

Lastly, he said to himself what was, he felt, the truth of this whole matter :

" When I am with her I am happy. But now I distort what is simple and drive myself crazy with false reasoning upon it."

Yet before he slept again he prayed, but though he had thought first to pray for guidance, in reality he prayed only that on the morrow he would see his vixen again and that God would preserve her, and her cubs too, from all dangers, and would allow him to see them often, so that he might come to love them for her sake as if he were their father, and that if this were a sin he might be forgiven, for he sinned in ignorance.

The next day or two he saw vixen and cubs again, though his visits were cut shorter, and these visits gave him such an innocent pleasure that very soon his notions of honour, duty and so on, were entirely forgotten, and his jealousy lulled asleep.

One day he tried taking with him the stereoscope and a pack of cards.

But though his Silvia was affectionate and amiable enough to let him put the stereoscope over her muzzle, yet she would not look through it, but kept turning her head to lick his hand, and it was plain to him that now she had quite forgotten the use of the instrument. It was the same too with the cards. For with them she was pleased enough, but only delighting to bite at them, and flip them about with her paws, and never considering for a moment whether they were diamonds or clubs, or hearts, or spades or whether the card was an ace or not. So it was evident that she had forgotten the nature of cards too.

Thereafter he only brought them things which she could better enjoy, that is sugar, grapes, raisins, and butcher's meat.

By-and-bye, as the summer wore on, the cubs came to know him, and he them, so that he was able to tell them easily apart, and then he christened them. For this purpose he brought a little bowl of water, sprinkled them as if in baptism and told them he was their godfather and gave each of them a name, calling them Sorel, Kasper, Selwyn, Esther, and Angelica.

Sorel was a clumsy little beast of a cheery and indeed puppyish disposition ; Kasper was fierce, the largest of the five, even in his play he would always bite, and gave his godfather many a sharp nip as time went on. Esther was of a dark complexion, a true brunette and very sturdy ; Angelica the brightest

72

red and the most exactly like her mother ; while Selwyn was the smallest cub, of a very prying, inquisitive and cunning temper, but delicate and undersized.

Thus Mr. Tebrick had a whole family now to occupy him, and, indeed, came to love them with very much of a father's love and partiality.

His favourite was Angelica (who reminded him so much of her mother in her pretty ways) because of a gentleness which was lacking in the others, even in their play. After her in his affections came Selwyn, whom he soon saw was the most intelligent of the whole litter. Indeed he was so much more quick-witted than the rest that Mr. Tebrick was led into speculating as to whether he had not inherited something of the human from his dam. Thus very early he learnt to know his name, and would come when he was called, and what was stranger still, he learnt the names of his brothers and sisters before they came to do so themselves.

Besides all this he was something of a young philosopher, for though his brother Kasper tyrannized over him he put up with it all with an unruffled temper. He was not, however, above playing tricks on the others, and one day when Mr. Tebrick was by, he made believe that there was a mouse in a hole some little way off. Very soon he was joined by Sorel, and presently by Kasper and Esther. When he had got them all digging, it was easy for him to slip away, and then he came to his godfather with a sly look, sat down before him, and smiled and then jerked his head over towards the others and smiled again and wrinkled his brows so that Mr. Tebrick knew as well as if he had spoken that the youngster was saying, " Have I not made fools of them all ? "

He was the only one that was curious about Mr. Tebrick ; he made him take out his watch, put his ear to it, considered it and wrinkled up his brows in perplexity. On the next visit it was the same thing. He must see the watch again, and again think over it. But clever as he was, little Selwyn could never understand it, and if his mother remembered anything about watches it was a subject which she never attempted to explain to her children.

One day Mr. Tebrick left the earth as usual and ran down the slope to the road, when he was surprised to find a carriage waiting before his house and a coachman walking about near his gate. Mr. Tebrick went in and found that his visitor was waiting for him. It was his wife's uncle.

They shook hands, though the Rev. Canon Fox did not recognise him immediately, and Mr. Tebrick led him into the house.

The clergyman looked about him a good deal, at the dirty and disorderly rooms, and when Mr. Tebrick took him into the drawing room it was evident that it had been unused for several months, the dust lay so thickly on all the furniture.

After some conversation on indifferent topics Canon Fox said to him :

" I have called really to ask about my niece."

Mr. Tebrick was silent for some time and then said :

" She is quite happy now."

" Ah—indeed. I have heard she is not living with you any longer."

" No. She is not living with me. She is not far away. I see her every day now."

" Indeed. Where does she live ? "

" In the woods with her children. I ought to tell you that she has changed her shape. She is a fox."

The Rev. Canon Fox got up ; he was alarmed, and everything Mr. Tebrick said confirmed what he had been led to expect he would find at Rylands. When he was outside, however, he asked Mr. Tebrick :

" You don't have many visitors now, eh ? "

" No—I never see anyone if I can avoid it. You are the first person I have spoken to for months."

" Quite right, too, my dear fellow. I quite understand—in the circumstances." Then the cleric shook him by the hand, got into his carriage and drove away.

" At any rate," he said to himself, " there will be no scandal." He was relieved also because Mr. Tebrick had said nothing about going abroad to disseminate the Gospel. Canon Fox had been alarmed by the letter, had not answered it, and thought that it was always better to let things be, and never to refer to anything unpleasant. He did not at all want to recommend Mr. Tebrick to the Bible Society if he were mad. His eccentricities would never be noticed at Stokoe. Besides that, Mr. Tebrick had said he was happy.

He was sorry for Mr. Tebrick too, and he said to

himself that the queer girl, his niece, must have married him because he was the first man she had met. He reflected also that he was never likely to see her again and said aloud, when he had driven some little way :

" Not an affectionate disposition," then to his coachman : " No, that's all right. Drive on, Hopkins."

When Mr. Tebrick was alone he rejoiced exceedingly in his solitary life. He understood, or so he fancied, what it was to be happy, and that he had found complete happiness now, living from day to day, careless of the future, surrounded every morning by playful and affectionate little creatures whom he loved tenderly, and sitting beside their mother, whose simple happiness was the source of his own.

" True happiness," he said to himself, " is to be found in bestowing love ; there is no such happiness as that of the mother for her babe, unless I have attained it in mine for my vixen and her children."

With these feelings he waited impatiently for the hour on the morrow when he might hasten to them once more.

When, however, he had toiled up the hillside, to the earth, taking infinite precaution not to tread down the bracken, or make a beaten path which might lead others to that secret spot, he found to his surprise that Silvia was not there and that there were no cubs to be seen either. He called to them, but it was in vain, and at last he laid himself on the mossy bank beside the earth and waited.

76

For a long while, as it seemed to him, he lay very
still, with closed eyes, straining his ears to hear every
rustle among the leaves, or any sound that might be
the cubs stirring in the earth.

At last he must have dropped asleep, for he woke
suddenly with all his senses alert, and opening his
eyes found a full-grown fox within six feet of him
sitting on its haunches like a dog and watching his
face with curiosity. Mr. Tebrick saw instantly that
it was not Silvia. When he moved the fox got up
and shifted his eyes, but still stood his ground, and
Mr. Tebrick recognised him then for the dog-fox
he had seen once before carrying a hare. It was the
same dark beast with a large white tag to his brush.
Now the secret was out and Mr. Tebrick could see
his rival before him. Here was the real father of his
godchildren, who could be certain of his taking
after him, and leading over again his wild and rakish
life. Mr. Tebrick stared for a long time at the handsome rogue, who glanced back at him with distrust
and watchfulness patent in his face, but not without
defiance too, and it seemed to Mr. Tebrick as if
there was also a touch of cynical humour in his look,
as if he said :

" By Gad ! we two have been strangely brought
together ! "

And to the man, at any rate, it seemed strange that
they were thus linked, and he wondered if the love
his rival there bare to his vixen and his cubs were
the same thing in kind as his own.

" We would both of us give our lives for theirs,"

he said to himself as he reasoned upon it, " we both of us are happy chiefly in their company. What pride this fellow must feel to have such a wife, and such children taking after him. And has he not reason for his pride ? He lives in a world where he is beset with a thousand dangers. For half the year he is hunted, everywhere dogs pursue him, men lay traps for him or menace him. He owes nothing to another."

But he did not speak, knowing that his words would only alarm the fox ; then in a few minutes he saw the dog-fox look over his shoulder, and then he trotted off as lightly as a gossamer veil blown in the wind, and, in a minute or two more, back he comes with his vixen and the cubs all around him. Seeing the dog-fox thus surrounded by vixen and cubs was too much for Mr. Tebrick ; in spite of all his philosophy a pang of jealousy shot through him. He could see that Silvia had been hunting with her cubs, and also that she had forgotten that he would come that morning, for she started when she saw him, and though she carelessly licked his hand, he could see that her thoughts were not with him.

Very soon she led her cubs into the earth, the dog-fox had vanished and Mr. Tebrick was again alone. He did not wait longer but went home.

Now was his peace of mind all gone, the happiness which he had flattered himself the night before he knew so well how to enjoy, seemed now but a fool's paradise in which he had been living. A hundred times this poor gentleman bit his lip, drew down his torvous brows, and stamped his foot, and cursed himself bitterly, or called his lady bitch. He could not forgive himself neither, that he had not thought of the damned dog-fox before, but all the while had let the cubs frisk round him, each one a proof that a dog-fox had been at work with his vixen. Yes, jealousy was now in the wind, and every circumstance which had been a reason for his felicity the night before was now turned into a monstrous feature of his nightmare. With all this Mr. Tebrick so worked upon himself that for the time being he had lost his reason. Black was white and white black, and he was resolved that on the morrow he would dig the vile brood of foxes out and shoot them, and so free himself at last from this hellish plague.

All that night he was in this mood, and in agony, as if he had broken in the crown of a tooth and bitten on the nerve. But as all things will have an ending so at last Mr. Tebrick, worn out and wearied by this loathed passion of jealousy, fell into an uneasy and tormented sleep.

After an hour or two the procession of confused and jumbled images which first assailed him passed away and subsided into one clear and powerful dream. His wife was with him in her own proper shape, walking as they had been on that fatal day before her transformation. Yet she was changed too, for in her face there were visible tokens of unhappiness, her face swollen with crying, pale and downcast, her hair hanging in disorder, her damp hands wringing a small handkerchief into a ball, her whole body shaken with sobs, and an air of long neglect about her person. Between her sobs she was confessing to him some crime which she had committed, but he did not catch the broken words, nor did he wish to hear them, for he was dulled by his sorrow. So they continued walking together in sadness as it were for ever, he with his arm about her waist, she turning her head to him and often casting her eyes down in distress.

At last they sat down, and he spoke, saying : " I know they are not my children, but I shall not use them barbarously because of that. You are still my wife. I swear to you they shall never be neglected. I will pay for their education."

Then he began turning over the names of schools in his mind. Eton would not do, nor Harrow, nor Winchester, nor Rugby. . . . But he could not tell why these schools would not do for these children of hers, he only knew that every school he thought of was impossible, but surely one could be found. So turning over the names of schools he sat for a long while holding his dear wife's hand, till at length, still weeping, she got up and went away and then slowly he awoke.

But even when he had opened his eyes and looked about him he was thinking of schools, saying to himself that he must send them to a private academy, or even at the worst engage a tutor. " Why, yes," he said to himself, putting one foot out of bed, " that is what it must be, a tutor, though even then there will be a difficulty at first."

At those words he wondered what difficulty there

would be and recollected that they were not ordinary children. No, they were foxes—mere foxes. When poor Mr. Tebrick had remembered this he was, as it were, dazed or stunned by the fact, and for a long time he could understand nothing, but at last burst into a flood of tears compassionating them and himself too. The awfulness of the fact itself, that his dear wife should have foxes instead of children, filled him with an agony of pity, and, at length, when he recollected the cause of their being foxes, that is that his wife was a fox also, his tears broke out anew, and he could bear it no longer but began calling out in his anguish, and beat his head once or twice against the wall, and then cast himself down on his bed again and wept and wept, sometimes tearing the sheets asunder with his teeth.

The whole of that day, for he was not to go to the earth till evening, he went about sorrowfully, torn by true pity for his poor vixen and her children.

At last when the time came he went again up to the earth, which he found deserted, but hearing his voice, out came Esther. But though he called the others by their names there was no answer, and something in the way the cub greeted him made him fancy she was indeed alone. She was truly rejoiced to see him, and scrambled up into his arms, and thence to his shoulder, kissing him, which was unusual in her (though natural enough in her sister Angelica). He sat down a little way from the earth fondling her, and fed her with some fish he had brought for her mother, which she ate so ravenously

that he concluded she must have been short of food that day and probably alone for some time.

At last while he was sitting there Esther pricked up her ears, started up, and presently Mr. Tebrick saw his vixen come towards them. She greeted him very affectionately but it was plain had not much time to spare, for she soon started back whence she had come with Esther at her side. When they had gone about a rod the cub hung back and kept stopping and looking back to the earth, and at last turned and ran back home. But her mother was not to be fobbed off so, for she quickly overtook her child and gripping her by the scruff began to drag her along with her.

Mr. Tebrick, seeing then how matters stood, spoke to her, telling her he would carry Esther if she would lead, so after a little while Silvia gave her over, and then they set out on their strange journey.

Silvia went running on a little before while Mr. Tebrick followed after with Esther in his arms whimpering and struggling now to be free, and indeed, once she gave him a nip with her teeth. This was not so strange a thing to him now, and he knew the remedy for it, which is much the same as with others whose tempers run too high, that is a taste of it themselves. Mr. Tebrick shook her and gave her a smart little cuff, after which, though she sulked, she stopped her biting.

They went thus above a mile, circling his house and crossing the highway until they gained a small covert that lay with some waste fields adjacent to it. And by this time it was so dark that it was all Mr. Tebrick could do to pick his way, for it was not always easy for him to follow where his vixen found a big enough road for herself.

But at length they came to another earth, and by the starlight Mr. Tebrick could just make out the other cubs skylarking in the shadows.

Now he was tired, but he was happy and laughed softly for joy, and presently his vixen, coming to him, put her feet upon his shoulders as he sat on the ground, and licked him, and he kissed her back on the muzzle and gathered her in his arms and rolled her in his jacket and then laughed and wept by turns in the excess of his joy.

All his jealousies of the night before were forgotten now. All his desperate sorrow of the morning and the horror of his dream were gone. What if they were foxes ? Mr. Tebrick found that he could be happy with them. As the weather was hot he lay out there all the night, first playing hide and seek with them in the dark till, missing his vixen and the cubs proving obstreperous, he lay down and was soon asleep.

He was woken up soon after dawn by one of the cubs tugging at his shoelaces in play. When he sat up he saw two of the cubs standing near him on their hind legs, wrestling with each other, the other two were playing hide and seek round a tree trunk, and now Angelica let go his laces and came romping into his arms to kiss him and say " Good morning " to him, then worrying the points of his waistcoat a little shyly after the warmth of his embrace.

That moment of awakening was very sweet to him. The freshness of the morning, the scent of everything at the day's rebirth, the first beams of the sun upon a tree-top near, and a pigeon rising into the air suddenly, all delighted him. Even the rough scent of the body of the cub in his arms seemed to him delicious.

At that moment all human customs and institutions seemed to him nothing but folly ; for said he, " I would exchange all my life as a man for my happiness now, and even now I retain almost all of the ridiculous conceptions of a man. The beasts are happier and I will deserve that happiness as best I can."

After he had looked at the cubs playing merrily, how, with soft stealth, one would creep behind another to bounce out and startle him, a thought came into Mr. Tebrick's head, and that was that these cubs were innocent, they were as stainless snow, they could not sin, for God had created them to be thus and they could break none of His commandments. And he fancied also that men sin because they cannot be as the animals.

Presently he got up full of happiness, and began

making his way home when suddenly he came to a full stop and asked himself : " What is going to happen to them ? "

This question rooted him stockishly in a cold and deadly fear as if he had seen a snake before him. At last he shook his head and hurried on his path. Aye, indeed, what would become of his vixen and her children ?

This thought put him into such a fever of apprehension that he did his best not to think of it any more, but yet it stayed with him all that day and for weeks after, at the back of his mind, so that he was not careless in his happiness as before, but as it were trying continually to escape his own thoughts.

This made him also anxious to pass all the time he could with his dear Silvia, and, therefore, he began going out to them for more of the daytime, and then he would sleep the night in the woods also as he had done that night ; and so he passed several weeks, only returning to his house occasionally to get himself a fresh provision of food. But after a week or ten days at the new earth both his vixen and the cubs, too, got a new habit of roaming. For a long while back, as he knew, his vixen had been lying out alone most of the day, and now the cubs were all for doing the same thing. The earth, in short, had served its purpose and was now distasteful to them, and they would not enter it unless pressed with fear.

This new manner of their lives was an added grief to Mr. Tebrick, for sometimes he missed them for hours together, or for the whole day even, and not

knowing where they might be was lonely and anxious.
Yet his Silvia was thoughtful for him too and would
often send Angelica or another of the cubs to fetch
him to their new lair, or come herself if she could
spare the time. For now they were all perfectly ac-
customed to his presence, and had come to look on
him as their natural companion, and although he
was in many ways irksome to them by scaring
rabbits, yet they always rejoiced to see him when they
had been parted from him. This friendliness of
theirs was, you may be sure, the source of most of
Mr. Tebrick's happiness at this time. Indeed he
lived now for nothing but his foxes, his love for his
vixen had extended itself insensibly to include her
cubs, and these were now his daily playmates so that
he knew them as well as if they had been his own
children. With Selwyn and Angelica indeed he was
always happy ; and they never so much as when they
were with him. He was not stiff in his behaviour
either, but had learnt by this time as much from his
foxes as they had from him. Indeed never was there
a more curious alliance than this or one with stranger
effects upon both of the parties.

Mr. Tebrick now could follow after them anywhere and keep up with them too, and could go
through a wood as silently as a deer. He learnt to
conceal himself if ever a labourer passed by so that
he was rarely seen, and never but once in their
company. But what was most strange of all, he had
got a way of going doubled up, often almost
on all fours with his hands touching the ground

86

every now and then, particularly when he went uphill.

He hunted with them too sometimes, chiefly by coming up and scaring rabbits towards where the cubs lay ambushed, so that the bunnies ran straight into their jaws.

He was useful to them in other ways, climbing up and robbing pigeon's nests for the eggs which they relished exceedingly, or by occasionally dispatching a hedgehog for them so they did not get the prickles in their mouths. But while on his part he thus altered his conduct, they on their side were not behindhand, but learnt a dozen human tricks from him that are ordinarily wanting in Reynard's education.

One evening he went to a cottager who had a row of skeps, and bought one of them, just as it was after the man had smothered the bees. This he carried to the foxes that they might taste the honey, for he had seen them dig out wild bees' nests often enough. The skep full was indeed a wonderful feast for them, they bit greedily into the heavy scented comb, their jaws were drowned in the sticky flood of sweetness, and they gorged themselves on it without restraint. When they had crunched up the last morsel they tore the skep in pieces, and for hours afterwards they were happily employed in licking themselves clean.

That night he slept near their lair, but they left him and went hunting. In the morning when he woke he was quite numb with cold, and faint with hunger. A white mist hung over everything and the wood smelt of autumn.

He got up and stretched his cramped limbs, and then walked homewards. The summer was over and Mr. Tebrick noticed this now for the first time and was astonished. He reflected that the cubs were fast growing up, they were foxes at all points, and yet when he thought of the time when they had been sooty and had blue eyes it seemed to him only yesterday. From that he passed to thinking of the future, asking himself as he had done once before what would become of his vixen and her children. Before the winter he must tempt them into the security of his garden, and fortify it against all the dangers that threatened them.

But though he tried to allay his fear with such resolutions he remained uneasy all that day. When

88

he went out to them that afternoon he found only
his wife Silvia there and it was plain to him that she
too was alarmed, but alas, poor creature, she could
tell him nothing, only lick his hands and face, and
turn about pricking her ears at every sound.

"Where are your children, Silvia?" he asked
her several times, but she was impatient of his ques-
tions, but at last sprang into his arms, flattened herself upon his breast and kissed him gently, so that
when he departed his heart was lighter because he
knew that she still loved him.

That night he slept indoors, but in the morning
early he was awoken by the sound of trotting horses,
and running to the window saw a farmer riding by
very sprucely dressed. Could they be hunting so
soon, he wondered, but presently reassured himself
that it could not be a hunt already.

He heard no other sound till eleven o'clock in the
morning when suddenly there was the clamour of
hounds giving tongue and not so far off neither. At
this Mr. Tebrick ran out of his house distracted and
set open the gates of his garden, but with iron bars
and wire at the top so the huntsmen could not follow.
There was silence again; it seems the fox must have
turned away, for there was no other sound of the
hunt. Mr. Tebrick was now like one helpless with
fear, he dared not go out, yet could not stay still at
home. There was nothing that he could do, yet he
would not admit this, so he busied himself in making
holes in the hedges, so that Silvia (or her cubs) could
enter from whatever side she came.

At last he forced himself to go indoors and sit down and drink some tea. While he was there he fancied he heard the hounds again ; it was but a faint ghostly echo of their music, yet when he ran out of the house it was already close at hand in the copse above.

Now it was that poor Mr. Tebrick made his great mistake, for hearing the hounds almost outside the gate he ran to meet them, whereas rightly he should have run back to the house. As soon as he reached the gate he saw his wife Silvia coming towards him but very tired with running and just upon her the hounds. The horror of that sight pierced him, for ever afterwards he was haunted by those hounds— their eagerness, their desperate efforts to gain on her, and their blind lust for her came at odd moments to frighten him all his life. Now he should have run back, though it was already late, but instead he cried out to her, and she ran straight through the open gate to him. What followed was all over in a flash, but it was seen by many witnesses.

The side of Mr. Tebrick's garden there is bounded by a wall, about six feet high and curving round, so that the huntsmen could see over this wall inside. One of them indeed put his horse at it very boldly, which was risking his neck, and although he got over safe was too late to be of much assistance.

His vixen had at once sprung into Mr. Tebrick's arms, and before he could turn back the hounds were upon them and had pulled them down. Then at that moment there was a scream of despair heard by all

the field that had come up, which they declared afterwards was more like a woman's voice than a man's. But yet there was no clear proof whether it was Mr. Tebrick or his wife who had suddenly regained her voice. When the huntsman who had leapt the wall got to them and had whipped off the hounds Mr. Tebrick had been terribly mauled and was bleeding from twenty wounds. As for his vixen she was dead, though he was still clasping her dead body in his arms.

Mr. Tebrick was carried into the house at once and assistance sent for, but there was no doubt now about his neighbours being in the right when they called him mad.

For a long while his life was despaired of, but at last he rallied, and in the end he recovered his reason and lived to be a great age, for that matter he is still alive.

FINIS.